D1079450
Once upon
a Pillar
Sherihan Achrafi
Illustrated By: Frances Espanol

ISBN: Softcover 978-1-5245-2051-9
Hardcover 978-1-5245-2052-6
EBook 978-1-5245-2071-7

Print information available on the last page

Rev. date: 12/12/2016

To order additional copies of this book, contact:
Xlibris
1-800-455-039
www.xlibris.com.au
Orders@Xlibris.com.au

Once Upon A Pillar

Sherihan Achrafi

Illustrated By: Frances Espanol

ONCE UPON
A PIL

Once upon a pillar, in a jungle far away lived Adam who didn't like himself very much. He felt sad and alone. But one day something special happened, and he became happier than ever. This is how he tells his story.

Oh, what I would give to fit in, to be free and beautiful and not be laughed at and teased for my fat, stubby legs.
I wanted to run and fly away, to find my own home. It felt almost impossible to be safe and alone.

I envied those who could fly, so free and relaxed, making their homes almost anywhere—the rain forest, field, prairie land, mountain tops, and desert sand.

I hated looking up to the world all the time. I was so small, and it was hard to be heard.

I hugged my warm green bedspread and nibbled on it for a few more minutes until I was satisfied.

The boys and girls ran around me; I felt exhausted just watching them.

"Come on, Adam; come and play hide-and-seek! Tip, you're in," said Beauty the Bird.
"I really can't, Beauty; I need to finish off my lunch," I replied.

"Oh, come on—unless you're too chicken," Penny the Penguin said, flapping his little hands at me.

"Fine ... I'm in. I'll count to ten. One ... two ..."
As I watched them run away and hide, I wondered.

I am rainbow in colour, yet short and stumpy.
My friends are fun and friendly.

I need some fresh air; I don’t belong anywhere.

"Eight ... nine ... ten!" I shouted, almost forgetting I was even playing.

I was so angry with myself.

So instead of finding my friends, I squirmed my body, avoiding the sticks and twigs in my way, until I found what I wanted to be my bedroom.

I grabbed a brown, silky blanket, so delicate and warm, protecting me from the outside world. I wrapped it around my entire body so tightly that I felt my stomach pound and my back muscles get squashed. Once I found my perfect position, I yawned and closed my small black eyes and prayed for a peaceful dream.

I watched the seasons pass by me from inside my shell. I witnessed how the autumn brown and orange leaves were blown away by the winter air and snow.

I patiently watched the white blanket that covered the green earth melt away from the blazing spring sun.

And then it was time to break free.

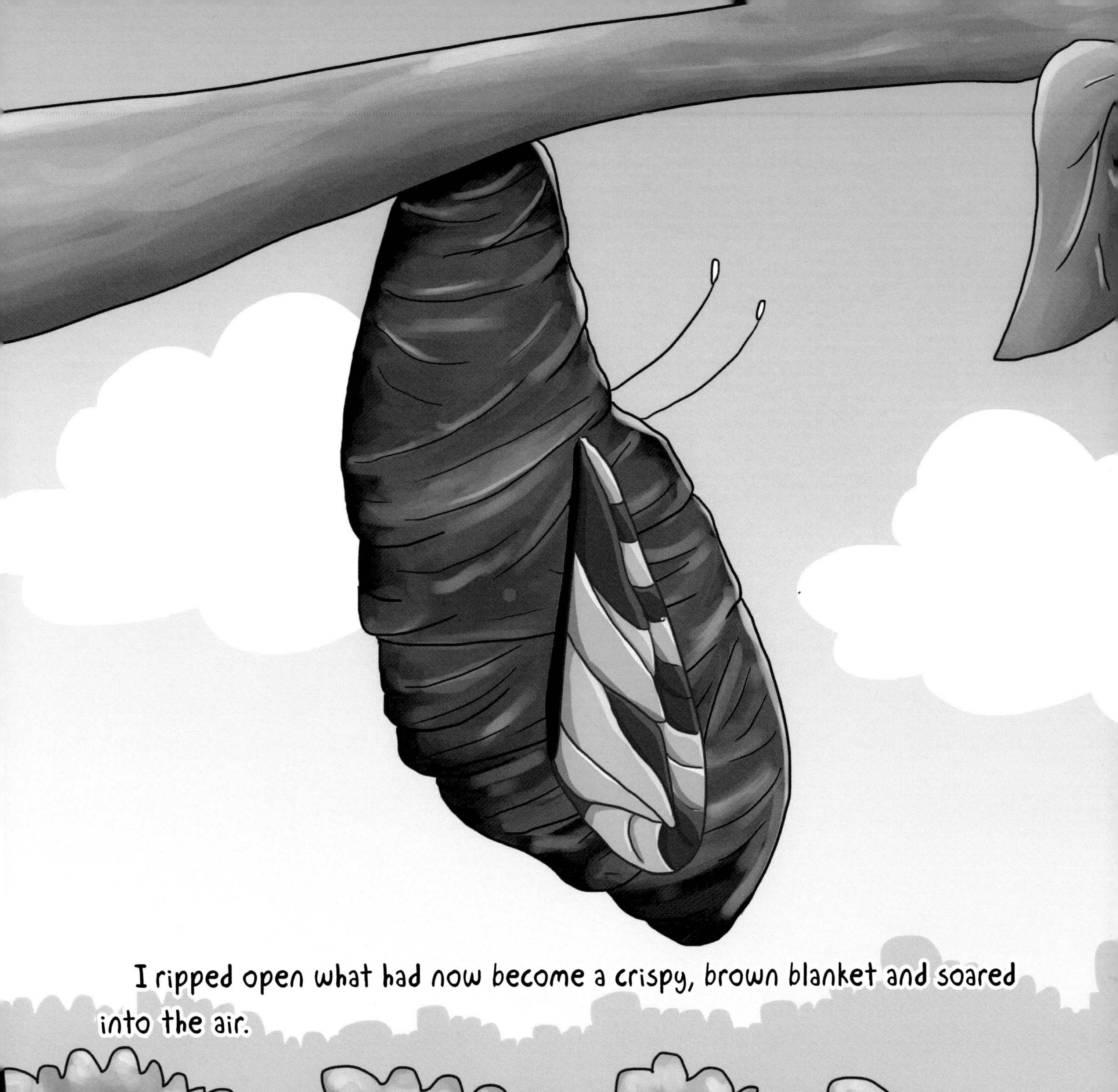

I ripped open what had now become a crispy, brown blanket and soared into the air.

I flew like an eagle across the horizon. Stretching my colourful wings into the free sky, I allowed the sun to take rest on my soft, beautiful, and delicate body.

I am the king of the sky!

I soared towards the broad blue beach, which smiled back at me. It reflected my features, which had somehow transformed from a clumsy and clueless caterpillar into a blossoming butterfly.

A group of butterflies that resembled me flew past. I felt accepted and at peace.

So I fluttered behind them and thought, I finally feel like I belong. *This is home, this is me, and I am free!*

ONCE UPON
A PILLAR

That's the tale of the little clumsy caterpillar. And he fluttered happily ever after.